For Marty and Ann McGovern Scheiner.
Without your beach and your love, I
couldn't have found the words.
For Lou Getoff,
a fine fellow who understands.
For lovely Belinda Langner,
my helping hand.

BY THE LIGHT OF THE SILVERY MOON   lyrics by Ed Madden, music by Gus Edwards
© 1909 JEROME H. REMICK & CO. © Renewed 1937 EDWIN H. MORRIS &
COMPANY, A Division of MPL Communications, Inc. International Copyright Secured.
All Rights Reserved. Used by Permission.

Library of Congress Cataloging in Publication Data   Langner, Nola. By the light of the
silvery moon.   Summary: Tired of always being told what to do, Mona goes out looking
for a powerful "King" who will be on her side and tell everyone else what to do.
[1. Self-reliance—Fiction.   2. Behavior—Fiction]   I. Title. PZ7.L268By 1983   [E]
82-12726 ISBN 0-688-01661-8 ISBN 0-688-01663-4 (lib. bdg.)

By the Light of the Silvery Moon

by Nola Langner

LOTHROP, LEE & SHEPARD BOOKS   NEW YORK

Someone who is good and kind and powerful. Someone in my house for me. Someone who is good and kind and powerful. Someone to take my side.

Mona loved to sing.
But not today.
Today she tramped around in the snow,
muttering to herself.
"They're always telling me what to do.
But can I tell them?
No."

It's not fair, said Mona. I need someone in my house for me.

Then Mona went right through the bushes
in the backyard.
She had never done that before.
That's funny, she thought,
I didn't even get a scratch.
Right away, she started to sing.

By the light of the silvery moon...

By the light of the silvery moon...

Mona walked and sang.
Suddenly she saw it.
A castle on top of the hill.
"I bet a King lives in there," said Mona.
"Kings always live in castles."
"Kings are the boss.
 They tell everybody what to do.
 They tell Mommies what to do.
 They tell Daddies what to do.
 But they never, ever tell me
 what to do.
 They are always on my side.

"That's it!" yelled Mona.
"That's what I need at home!
 Just for me—a King."

And Mona ran up to the top
of the hill.

A handsome knight stood
in front of the castle.
He had a big sword.
"Good morrow, good maiden,"
said the knight.
"How goest thou?"

"Not so hot," said Mona.
"I'm looking for a King.
  I need one in my house.
  Perchance you are one?" she asked the knight.

"Indeed I am," said the knight.
"I am King of all the Dragonslayers
  in the kingdom—and probably in the
  whole wide world."

"Oh, swell," said Mona.
"Then you can come
  home with me.
  Tonight is meatballs,
  I like a lot of catsup, don't you?

And after supper we'll watch my favorite
shows. *Frankenstein, Bride of Frankenstein,*
and *Frankenstein's Revenge.*
Then we can sing some songs.
I love to sing, don't you?"

By the light of the silvery moon...

"Whoa," said the knight.
"Holdest thou your horses, prithee.
  Forsooth," he said,
"I've still got a dynasty of dragons to kill.
  Forgive me, fair damsel, I cannot come home with you."
  He bowed—a fine, knightly bow.

"Can I help?" asked Mona.
"Well, come to think of it, mayhap," said the knight.
  He mounted his horse.
"Jumpest up behind me," he said to Mona,
"and hangest on."

  When it was over, the knight said,
"Methinks it was a jolly good try."
"No offense, Your Knighthood," said Mona.
"But I think I'll be moving along."
  She bowed low and skipped away.
"Alas, alack," called the knight. "Will you be back?"
  From far away came Mona's answer.

By the light of the silvery...

Mona walked for a long time.
She saw a great big cowboy.
"Howdy, you cute li'l varmint," he said.
He smiled a great big cowboy smile.
"Whatchouall doin' in these here parts?"
"I'm looking for a King," said Mona.
"And I sure am hoping you're one."

"Well, you purty little tumbleweed,
Meet the King of all the Cowboys, that's me."
And he smiled another great big cowboy smile.

"Oh, good," said Mona.
"Then you can come home with me."

"Jest one cotton-pickin' minute, little lady,"
 said the cowboy.
"I'm doin' some serious cowpoking here.
 I can't just leave my cows."
 And he smiled another great big cowboy smile.

 Mona smiled back.
"Maybe I could lend a hand?" she said.
"Well, my darlin'," said the cowboy,
"maybe you could.
 Jest grab aholt of this rope."

"I think I'll be moseying on," said Mona.
"It's time to hit the trail.
  I believe I hear someone calling me now."

"Well, hush my puppies," said the cowboy.
"If that ain't too bad.
  I'll miss you, honey chile."
  Mona walked into the sunset.
  The cowboy played her a little song.

  And Mona sang back,

Mona kept on walking.
She walked through a big gate.
There was a lot of noise.

A man was running around a stage
with different instruments.
He was trying to play them all at once.
Maybe he's not too bad when he's not so nervous,
Mona thought.
"Are you a King?" she asked him.

"You bet your bongos I'm a King.
The King of Rock."
He turned around.
"Hey, you're a pretty foxy chick," he said.
"Thanks," said Mona.
"Would you come home with me?"

"Funky. Very funky," said the King of Rock.
"How can I come home with you?
  I don't even have a group."

"I could be your group," said Mona.
  She sat down behind the drums.
"Coolamundo," said the King of Rock.
"Roll me a riff."
  Mona rolled a gorgeous riff,
  and sang her favorite song.
  She banged the drums
  and finished with a paradiddle.

"Was I cool?" she asked.
"What's with you, kid?" moaned the King.
"You a looney tune, or what?
  Go work some other gig, Babe.
  Don't bust my chops."

"I dig," said Mona.
   She jumped off the stage.
"I guess it's time to split."

After him, even home looks good, thought Mona.
"Oh well," she said.
"I guess we all have our problems."

"Even kings," said a fuzzy voice.
"What? Huh? Who?
 Who said that?"
 Mona jumped around.

"Whatsa matter," asked the small voice,
"you blind or something?
 Can't see what's right in front of your face,
 for goodness' sake?
 Look down in the grass, silly.
 Third daisy from the left."

It was a Magic Bee.
It was wearing a crown.

"Wow," said Mona.
"Are you the King of Bees or something?"
 To herself she thought, *Enough's enough.*
 I'm not asking this one to come home.

"No, dummy," said the Bee. "I'm the Queen.
 Queen of all the Bees in the whole wide world.
 And I wouldn't come home with you,
 Not even for a truckload of
 Pennsylvania Purple Clover Supreme.
 Listen to me," she said to Mona.

"You wouldn't know a bathtub of
 honey if you fell in it.

I'm a regular Queen Bee, and I'm
gonna give you some good advice.
So listen up.

"Keep on sticking up for yourself.
You've been doing it all along.
Kid, you don't need no King, no Queen—
you've got yourself.

"So go home to your folks, who love you.
Whatsa matter with you?
Staying away from home so long
and making everyone crazy."

It was snowing.
But Mona felt warm all over.
"Yeah," she said "That's right.
I can stick up for myself.
I can be on my own side."

She waved goodbye to the Queen. Then she ran back through the bushes.

Her mother and father were waiting.

Everybody hugged Everybody.